For Joshua   FP
Pour Alphée   CR

VIKING
Published by the Penguin Group
Viking Penguin, a division of Penguin Books USA Inc.,
375 Hudson Street, New York, New York 10014, U.S.A.
Penguin Books Australia Ltd, Ringwood, Victoria, Australia
Penguin Books Canada Ltd, 2801 John Street, Markham, Ontario, Canada L3R 1B4
Penguin Books (N.Z.) Ltd, 182-190 Wairau Road, Auckland 10, New Zealand

This edition first published in Great Britain by ABC, 1990
First American edition published in 1991

1   3   5   7   9   10   8   6   4   2

Text copyright © Felix Pirani, 1990
Illustrations copyright © Christine Roche, 1990

All rights reserved

Library of Congress catalog number: 90-50075

ISBN 0-670-83375-4

Printed in Great Britain
by MacLehose & Partners for Imago

Triplets

By Felix Pirani

Illustrated by Christine Roche

VIKING

Once upon a time there were three little girls called Rosie, Susie and Tracy. They were about six years old, and they were triplets.

Sisters or brothers who are all born at the same
time from the same mother are called

twins if there are two of them,

triplets if there are three of them,

quadruplets if there are four of them,

quintuplets if there are five of them,

sextuplets if there are six of them.

There aren't usually more than six at once. At least not for people. There are for some animals.

Rosie, Susie and Tracy's mother sometimes called them R, S and T, for short.

All of Rosie's T-shirts had R on them, and all of Susie's T-shirts had S on them, and all of Tracy's T-shirts had T on them.

Their jeans, shoes, socks and bathing suits were marked the same way. Some of their toys were for everybody, and some of them were marked R or S or T.

Rosie, Susie and
Tracy all looked
exactly alike.

Of course, they knew which was which,
and their mother and father knew which
was which, but their grandmother wasn't
always sure, and their aunts and uncles
weren't always sure,

and their teacher, who was
called Mr. Jones, was
hardly ever sure,

because they hadn't been in his class very
long, so he didn't know them very well. So
the only way he could tell them apart was
by the R's, S's and T's on their clothes.

Rosie, Susie and Tracy didn't mind
if people mixed them up.

They thought it was funny.

Their grandmother came into the bathroom one day when they were having their baths. They hadn't any T-shirts on and hadn't any bathing suits on. In fact, they hadn't anything on at all. Their grandmother said to the one in the bath, "Hello. Are you Susie?" and the one in the bath said, "No, I'm Tracy," and the one who was drying herself said, "I'm Susie!" and then the triplets all laughed and their grandmother laughed too.

She couldn't see any little differences to tell them apart. Of course, there were big differences being Rosie or Susie or Tracy, but not much for other people to see.

One morning, Susie said to Rosie and Tracy, "Let's get really mixed up and see what happens."
Rosie said, "We could trade T-shirts."
Tracy said, "We could trade jeans, too!"

So Rosie put on a T-shirt with S on it and jeans with T on them, and Susie put on a T-shirt with T on it and jeans with R on them, and Tracy put on a T-shirt with R on it and jeans with S on them.

When they went to breakfast their mother said, "You're all mixed up!" and laughed.

"It's only for fun," they said.

After breakfast their mother said, "This morning we're all going to the dentist." And off they went.

The dentist said, "Let's see, who
shall we have first? Rosie first.
Then Susie and then Tracy.
Which is Rosie?"

Tracy said, "I'm Rosie," because she had R on her T-shirt but then Susie said, "No, I'm Rosie," because she had R on her jeans, and then Rosie said, "No, I'm Rosie," because she was.

The dentist said, "It doesn't matter who comes first, even if you're all Rosie. You come first."

And he pointed to Tracy.

So Tracy sat in the dentist's chair
and the dentist looked into her mouth.

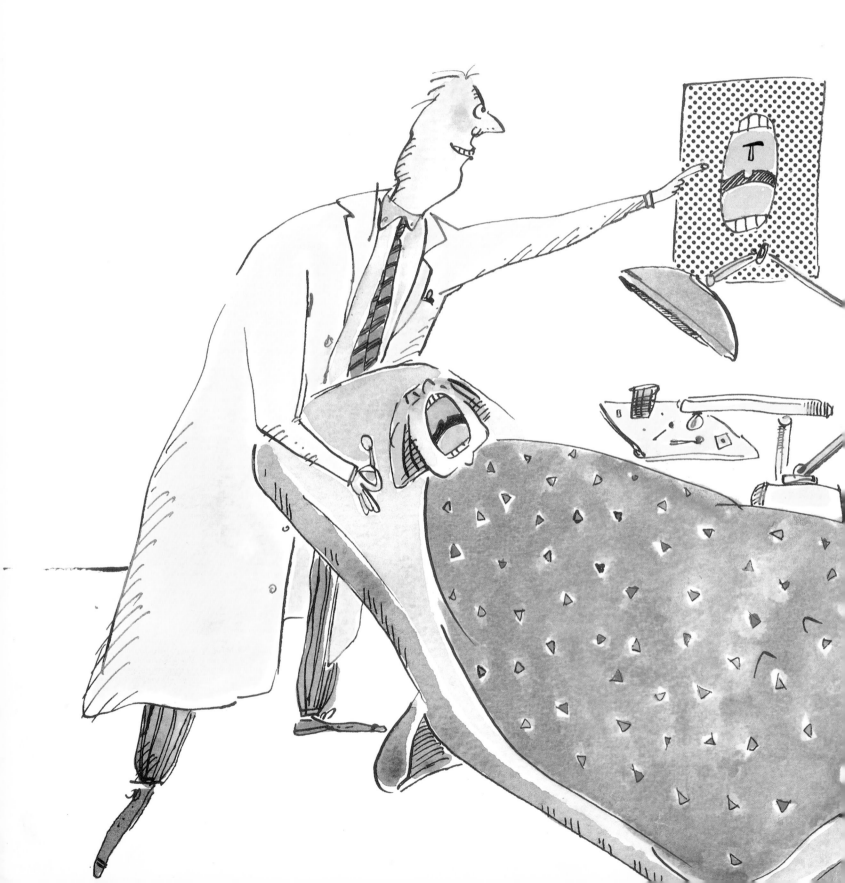

Then he looked at the three charts for the three triplets, and he said, "You're Tracy."

Tracy said, "Yes. How do you know?"

 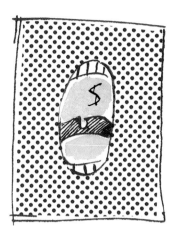

The dentist said, "This is your chart, which shows all your teeth; it's like a map of your mouth, and it has marks on it to show where your second teeth are, and where your fillings are if you have any, and your second teeth are in the wrong places for you to be Rosie or Susie, and in the right places for you to be Tracy, so you must be Tracy."

And then he looked all around Tracy's mouth, and pushed and poked, but it was all right and Tracy didn't have to have any fillings.

Then the dentist pointed to
Susie and said, "You next,"

and when he looked at Susie's mouth he said, "You're Susie," and Susie said, "Yes," and her teeth were all right too. So were Rosie's.

Then they all went home again.

Their mother said, "Now, I want you to put on the right T-shirts and jeans, because I know which is which and the dentist knows which is which but lots of people don't and it's time to go to school and you mustn't confuse Mr. Jones."

So Rosie took off her T-shirt and gave it to Susie, and took off her jeans and gave them to Tracy, and Susie took off her T-shirt and gave it to Tracy, and took off her jeans

and gave them to Rosie, and Tracy took off her T-shirt and gave it to Rosie, and took off her jeans and gave them to Susie, and they all put on the right clothes . . .

...and went to school and had a lovely day,
being themselves.

E
Pirani, Felix.
Triplets

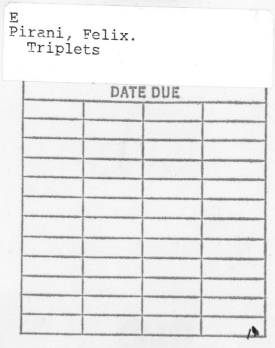

DATE DUE

11/91